Cross On A Chain

(Inspired by True Events)

Irene Kueh

This is a work of fiction. Names, characters, businesses, places, events and incidents are either the products of the author's imagination or used in a fictitious manner. Any resemblance to actual persons, living or dead, or actual events is purely coincidental.

ISBN: 9798663691994

Dedicated to YOU

(each and every one of you)

We can achieve Peace
If we ask Peace be the Guardian of our actions

One

"I can't believe this!" Logan Spencer yelled.

The wheel of his car grinded into the asphalt before coming to a stop on the side of the road. He stepped out. The back tire deflated before his eyes. He stared at the cloudless sky and fisted his palms.

"What have I done to be at the receiving end of your wrath?" His eyes burned with hot tears. "Have I not suffered enough?"

He popped the trunk, and his blood boiled over. His brother borrowed his spare tire and hadn't returned it to him. He kicked the back tire and grabbed his keys. With a big groan, he locked his car and started walking.

The sun did not have any sympathy for him either. Sweat dripped from his forehead and ran down his back. He still had a couple more miles to go. Cars drove by without stopping.

He wondered if the roles were reversed, would he stop? Most probably not. He wiped his face with his drenched sleeve. After a while, he stopped looking at the cars passing by. A car slowed beside him. Still, he didn't bother to look.

"Logan," a familiar voice called out.

Logan turned.

Jason Flynn, his brother's friend, stopped his car and rolled down the window. "Hey, what happened? I thought I saw your car back there."

Logan glanced over his shoulder. He couldn't see his silver car. "Yeah… Flat tire."

"Hop on in," said Jason.

"Thank you," said Logan as he got into the car. "Markus borrowed my spare last week and forgot to return it to me." He felt guilty for blaming his brother. He quickly added, "And I forgot to ask."

Jason made a U-turn. "I got a spare. Let's get your car fixed up." He turned up the air. "How's Markus? I haven't talked to him lately."

"I hardly see him myself," said Logan. "He's busy with his girlfriend."

Jason parked behind Logan's car. "Blame it on love."

Logan smiled. Although his girlfriend dumped him exactly a year ago, he was happy for his younger brother, Markus. After a few minutes, they changed the tire.

"Thank you so much, Jason," said Logan. "I owe you one."

"Don't mention it," said Jason.

"Are you staying at your parents this summer?" asked Logan.

"Yeah," said Jason. "You?"

"Same," said Logan. "I'll return your tire in the next day or so."

Jason made an Okay sign with his fingers. "Sounds good. Drive safe." He waved and drove away.

Logan started his car and followed suit. As they reached the fork of the road, Jason honked and turned right. Logan honked twice and went in the opposite direction.

Two

Although Logan had a key to his parents' home, he knocked. His father opened the door.

"You're late," said his father. "Your mother's worried."

"Sorry, Dad," said Logan. "I had a flat tire." He looked around. "Where's Mom?"

"Where else," said his father.

Logan nodded. Not a day went by that his mother did not go in The Room. He headed toward the back. The door was open. His mother stood in front of the shrine. In her hand was a gold lid.

When he was a young boy, he used to play in The Room. There was nothing else in there but a beautiful oak wood shelf mounted on the wall. He was too short to reach it, but there was a small gold jar sitting on the shelf. As he grew older, he realized it was his mother's sacred room.

Without looking at him, his mother spoke. "I'm glad you're home safe," she said. "Come in."

Logan entered in silent. His mother took the jar from the shrine and handed it to Logan. He took it and rubbed the beautiful scroll motif on the jar. Knowing well there was nothing inside the jar, still he peered inside.

"It's been a while," he said to himself. "Thank you for keeping me safe."

"Yes, thank you." His mother took the jar and put it back on the shrine. "Why are you home so late?"

Logan took a deep breath. He was getting tired of repeating the same thing. "I had a flat tire."

"Oh my, good thing Markus returned your spare in time," she said.

"Actually, he didn't," said Logan.

His mother's face darkened. "How did you get home? Did you walk?"

Logan cringed. As much as he wanted to chew out Markus, he didn't want to involve their mother. "Jason saw me and let me use his spare."

"Ah, bless him," his mother said. Her eyes were on the gold jar. "Bless you, Jason." She faced Logan. "I'll have a serious talk with Markus."

"It's okay, Mom," he said. "Don't be too hard on him. His mind is occupied."

His mother glared at him. "This is too much."

Logan winced. The look on his mother's face scared the life out of him. He had to warn Markus ASAP.

"Where are you, Markus?" asked Logan. He didn't mean to say it out loud.

"That's a silly question," she said.

"Yikes," he whispered. "I need to clean up."

"All right," she said. "Dinner will be ready soon."

"Thanks, Mom."

"Close the door behind you."

His mother faced the shrine once more. Logan closed the door and walked away. He grabbed his phone from his pocket and sent his brother a text message.

"Get Mom some flowers and come home."

In an instant, his phone rang.

Before he could say hello, his brother spoke. "What's going on? You're scaring me."

"I had a flat tire." Logan was getting sick of saying it over and over.

"Oh no," said Markus. "I still have your spare. Where are you? I'll come and get you now."

"I'm home," said Logan. "Mom is not too happy."

Markus let out a loud sigh. "Oh man, you should have called me."

"My phone's dead and I didn't have my charger in the car," said Logan.

"I'm so sorry," said Markus. "How far did you have to walk?"

"I was sweating buckets," said Logan. "Thankfully, Jason drove by and saw me."

"Aah, how's my good old pal?" asked Markus.

"He looks good," said Logan. He heard sound of footsteps. "I'm going to hit the shower and you better come home ALONE. And seriously, get Mom something."

"I'm leaving now," said Markus. "Thanks, Bro."

Logan sprinted toward the bathroom and locked the door.

Three

Markus Spencer screeched to a halt in front of the house. He ran out with a bouquet of daisies, his mother's favorite. His hands were shaky and clammy. Yes, he felt guilty for what happened to his brother, but he was more petrified of his mother. Before he could knock, Logan opened the door.

"How's Mom?" asked Markus.

"She has calmed down a little." Logan nodded at the flowers. "Good choice."

Markus stared at the flowers in his hand. "I hope this helps. Oh, I have your spare in my trunk." He handed his car key to Logan.

Logan took the key and walked down the stairs.

"Hold up! Can you wait for a bit?" asked Markus.

Logan turned. "Why?"

Markus raised the flowers. "Let me give these to Mom first."

Logan scratched the side of his head. Should he help his brother? He knew Markus wanted to give the daisies to their mother and dashed outside as fast as he could. It sounded funny but he'd do the same.

"Come on, help me out here," said Markus.

Logan smiled. "Fine, go ahead."

Markus stepped inside the house. His parents were not in the living room. The sound of cutlery clinking against the dishes made him a little woozy. He took a deep breath and crept toward the kitchen.

"*Come on, Markus*," his little inner voice whispered. "*There's nothing to be afraid of.*"

Markus entered the kitchen. "Hi, Mom. Hi, Dad."

His parents turned.

"Welcome home, Markus," said his father.

Before his mother said a word, he handed the daisies to his mother. "For you, Mom."

His mother narrowed her eyes at him and let out a sigh.

The smell of caramel hit his nostrils. He looked at the caramel pie. "Smells good, Mom."

"These are beautiful." His mother took the daisies. "Are you hungry?"

As much as he wanted to eat, he needed to get out of the kitchen. "In a bit, Mom. I want to help Logan."

That earned him another glare from his mother. Before his mother gave him a lash, he raced out.

Logan leaned against the trunk with a quirky smile. "You survived…"

"Not funny," said Markus.

Logan threw Markus's key back to him. "I need to get a new tire."

Logan had taken the tire out from Markus's trunk and it was lying next to Logan's car.

"I'll go with you," said Markus.

"I'll manage," said Logan.

"No, I need to go with you," said Markus.

Logan chuckled. "Chicken."

"You'd be too," said Markus.

"Fine," said Logan. "Go tell Mom."

It was Markus turn to give Logan a glare. "Again, not funny."

Logan laughed and ran upstairs. "Mom, Dad, Markus and I are going out."

A few minutes later, Logan came out. "Mom said make sure you pay for it."

Without missing a beat, Markus nodded. "Deal."

"Wow, what gets into you?" asked Logan.

"I feel guilty, man," said Markus.

"You should be," said Logan. "It was excruciating. I was sweating bullets."

"I'm sorry. I'll make it up to you," said Markus.

Logan laughed. "I'm messing with you." He started the car and drove away.

Four

After a few hours, Logan got a new tire on his car and to his surprise, Markus paid for it.

"You don't have to do that," said Logan.

"I owe you, remember," said Markus.

"You owe me nothing," said Logan.

Markus ignored him and made a call. "Hey Jason," he said. "Thank you for helping Logan… Are you home?" After a few seconds, Markus added, "Great, Logan and I will be there soon. Thanks again, man." Markus ended the call. "Jason is on his way home."

"Okay," said Logan.

Logan knew where Jason lived but he had never been inside the ranch-style house. He turned right at the fork of the road and before long, a lime green house came to view. Three cars were parked in the driveway.

"It looks like everyone's home," said Markus.

Sweat started to bead on Logan's forehead. He looked around. "We should come back."

"Don't be silly," said Markus. "They're nice folks."

"I didn't say they're not," said Logan.

"They are the friendliest family," said Markus. "Besides, you know Jason and his parents."

"But I don't know his sisters," said Logan.

Markus chuckled. "Sofia and Ashley are nice." Before Logan could protest, his brother added, "We won't stay long."

That calmed Logan. They stepped out. A red barn on the back of the house caught Logan's eyes. Whenever he drove by, he would always look at it. "I like the barn."

"Same here," said Markus.

Jason stepped out the front door. "Hey Markus," he said. "Hey Logan."

"Hey Jason," said Logan. "I got your spare tire."

"Give me a sec," Jason said and went back inside the house. He stepped out a few seconds later. "I see you got a new one."

"Yeah," said Logan. "Thank you again for your help."

Jason waved his hand. "Don't mention it." He popped the trunk.

Logan did the same and took out the tire and put it into Jason's.

"Everyone's home, huh," said Markus.

"Yeah, Sofia and Ashley had just arrived this afternoon," said Jason. "You called at the right time. We were just leaving the church."

Markus nodded. "I'm good like that."

Logan shook his head. "Ignore him."

Jason smiled. "Why don't you come inside," he said.

Logan looked at Markus.

"You haven't been here for a while, Markus," said Jason.

Feeling indebted to Jason, Logan didn't see any other option. "All right, we'll stay for a bit."

"Great," said Jason. "Come on in." He held the door open.

For unknown reasons, Logan's heartbeat raced.

"Hey Markus," said Jason's parents.

"Long time no see, Logan," said Jason's father.

Logan remembered Jason's father as a jokester. He smiled. "Hi Mike."

"How are your parents?" asked Beth, Jason's mother.

"They're good, Beth," said Logan. "How are you both?"

"We're fine," said Beth. She left and returned with some drinks. "Have some tea. Mike and I are going to the barn. We'll talk to you later."

"Okay," said Logan. "Thank you."

Jason's parents left and a female voice filled the air. "Hey Markus."

A young brunette woman stepped into the living room. Unlike Jason's wavy hair, hers was straight and long.

"Hey Sofia," said Markus. "How've you been?"

"Glad it's summer," said Sofia.

"About time, right," said Markus.

Sofia turned toward Logan. For a second, Logan's heart skipped a beat.

"Hi," she said.

Logan cleared his throat. "Hi," he said.

"That's Logan," said Jason. "Markus's brother."

"Oh," said Sofia. "Nice meeting you, Logan."

Not knowing how to answer, Logan simply smiled.

"How's life, Markus?" asked Sofia.

Logan knew Markus and Jason were friends from high school. He didn't know he was close to Jason's family.

"Life's great," said Markus. "Is Ashley home?"

"Yeah, she's in her room," said Sofia. "How about you, Logan?"

All of a sudden, Logan clammed up. He opened his mouth, but nothing came out.

Markus stared at him. "You okay?"

Again, Logan cleared his throat. "I… I'm fine." He felt he needed to say more and added, "Your brother saved my life this morning."

"Really?" Sofia's eyes brightened. "What did my brother do?"

"Just as I drove on the main road, I had a flat tire," said Logan. This time, he gladly repeated the story. "Jason stopped and helped me out."

"Thank goodness," she said. "That's a long walk home."

Logan chuckled. "Yes, it is." He looked around. Markus and Jason were nowhere to be found. For some strange reason, he didn't mind. Sofia was very good at making him feel comfortable.

Markus and Jason reappeared.

"Hey Logan, can you help Jason with his computer?' asked Markus.

"Sure." Logan stood. "I'd be happy to."

"You don't have to do it now," said Jason. "Just when you're free."

"Definitely," said Logan.

"It's getting late," said Markus. "Thanks again for helping my bro."

"Yes, thank you," said Logan.

"Don't mention it," said Jason.

From the corner of his eye, Logan looked at Sofia. She was watching the news. "I can come tomorrow if you're free," he said.

"That's awesome," said Jason. "Markus has my number. Call or text me."

"I will," said Logan.

Sofia glanced over her shoulder. "Are you leaving?"

Markus rubbed his stomach. "Yeah, I'm hungry."

"Why didn't you say something?" asked Sofia. "We have food, you know."

"Do you have caramel apple pie?" asked Markus.

"That we don't," said Sofia.

Markus frowned. "Then, I must leave," he said.

"How rude," said Logan.

"She knows I'm kidding," said Markus.

Sofia let out the most melodious laugh.

"See you guys later," said Markus.

Sofia waved her long slender fingers. Her bright red nails entranced him. "Nice meeting you, Logan."

"Nice meeting you too, Sofia," said Logan.

Logan and Markus bade their farewells and left.

"They're nice," said Logan as he unlocked his car.

"I told you," said Markus.

"Jason has two sisters, right?" asked Logan.

"Yeah," said Markus. "Don't take it personally. Once you get to know Ashley, she'll be your best friend."

"Hmm…"

Markus smiled. "I know what you're thinking. Ashley's an introvert. The total opposite of Jason and Sofia. But she's really nice."

"*Sofia is nice*," Logan said to himself. He couldn't wait to see her again.

Five

Sofia Flynn had known Markus for as long as she could remember. She had only heard of Logan and seen pictures of him through Markus. This night was the first time she talked to Logan.

"Logan seems nice," said Sofia to Jason.

"Yes, he is," said Jason. "I'm glad he can help me with my computer."

"Now, you can save your money for your games," said Sofia.

They laughed.

"What's so funny?" asked Ashley, as she entered the living room.

"Markus's brother is going to help Jason with his computer problem," said Sofia. "Now he can buy his games."

Ashley smiled. "Where are Mom and Dad?"

"Where else?" asked Sofia.

"They sure love their toys," said Ashley.

Their parents had just bought a camper. They were ready to spend their summer outdoor. Even Ashley, her hermit sister, was looking forward to it.

"You should have come out and joined us earlier." said Sofia. "Logan is nice, like Markus."

Ashley sat down beside her. "How's Markus?"

"He looks great," said Sofia.

"He has a girlfriend," said Jason.

"Good for him," said Ashley.

Jason's phone beeped. "Logan said he can come tomorrow." He typed something and grinned. "Yes, yes, yes."

Ashley smiled. "Now you can stop worrying about it."

"I should get some wings or something," said Jason.

"Now I'm hungry," said Ashley.

"Join us tomorrow," said Jason.

"Is Markus coming?" asked Ashley.

"Yeah," said Jason.

"All right," said Ashley. "Save me some wings."

* ~ | ~ | ~ * | * ~ | ~ | ~ *

Ashley Flynn sat on her bed with her eyes fixed on the altar. Her father had built the wall-mounted altar the day she was born. The picture of Virgin Mary and Jesus seemed to be looking right back at her.

"It's good to be home," said Ashley. "I've missed you."

She squished her plush pillow against her back.

"Thank you for keeping my parents, Jason, and Sofia safe. Continue to watch over us, Lord."

She picked up her Rosary from the end table. She ran her fingers over the beads and made the sign of the cross. She closed her eyes and prayed. Every bead touched her soul. She breathed in every word.

After the first decade, Ashley lay back down and closed her eyes. Her lips kept praying until she fell asleep.

The following day, Logan stopped by. Ashley stayed in her room. She was reading her favorite Book of Saints, when someone knocked on her door.

"Ashley, the wings are here," said Jason.

"Okay, I'll be out in a bit," said Ashley.

After half an hour, Ashley closed her book and stepped out.

In the kitchen, Jason, Sofia, and Logan sat around the dinner table.

"Have some," said Jason.

"Hi Ashley," said Logan.

Ashley studied Logan. Unlike Markus's long caramel brown hair, Logan hair was short light chestnut brown. "You must be Logan."

Logan smiled. "Yes, nice to meet you."

"Nice to meet you too," said Ashley. "Where's Markus?"

"He went to see his girlfriend," said Logan.

"Aah." Ashley sat down. "Where are Mom and Dad?"

"Where else," said Jason.

Ashley smiled. Two bowls of wings were on the table. Jason grabbed a couple wings and placed them on his plate. Logan was talking to Sofia instead of eating.

"Don't worry about Mom and Dad," said Jason. "I saved some for them."

"Great," said Ashley, as she took a few wings and put them on her plate. She took a bite. "This is good."

"Yes, it is," said Logan.

"Did you fix Jason's computer?" asked Ashley.

"He sure did," said Sofia. "He's going to look at my laptop next."

"That's good,' said Ashley.

"If you want me to look at your computer, let me know," said Logan.

"Thank you," said Ashley. She stayed in the kitchen for a while before she licked her fingers and stood up. "I'm going to watch some TV."

"We'll join you in a bit," said Sofia. Hot sauce dripped from her mouth.

Ashley pointed to her lips. Sofia took her napkin and wiped her mouth. She put the dishes in the sink, washed her hands, and walked into the living room.

Six

Logan came to the house every day for the whole week. Jason entered Ashley's room.

Jason bounced a Rubik's Cube in his hands. "Hey, you got a sec?"

Ashley set aside her book. "Sure, what's up?"

Jason grabbed a chair and sat down. "Have you noticed Logan coming by every day?"

"Yeah, he seems nice," she said.

Jason scrambled up the Cube.

Ashley pointed at the Cube. "You're driving me nuts. I can't ever figure it out."

"I offered to teach you…"

Ashley shook her head. "It's hopeless."

Jason put down his cube on the table. "Anyway, do you think Logan is spending a lot of time with Sofia?"

Ashley tilted her head side to side. "Hmm… yes."

"So, you noticed it too?" he asked.

"I'm not blind, Jason," she said. "Does it bother you?"

Jason chuckled. "I'm a little worried."

Ashley narrowed her eyes at her brother. "Why?"

"He likes Sofia," said Jason. "But Sofia treats him as a friend… as Markus's brother. Logan got hurt bad before. His girlfriend dumped him."

Ashley took a deep breath. "Have you talked to Sofia?"

"Are you crazy?" asked Jason.

Ashley smiled. "I'll talk to her."

"I don't want to make it awkward," said Jason. "Maybe we should just let this one play itself out."

"Sounds good," said Ashley.

Jason's phone beeped. He read something on the screen and looked up. "You won't believe this." He raised his phone.

Ashley read it. "Hey Jason, can I go to church with you this Sunday?" She nodded. "Say yes."

"His family is going to have a cow," said Jason.

"They are Christians, aren't they?" asked Ashley.

"They don't practice," said Jason.

"Well, what are you going to say to him?" asked Ashley.

"I can't say no," said Jason. He typed something and put down his phone. "Done."

"Where's Sofia?" asked Ashley.

"Out with friends," said Jason.

"I should go to the barn," said Ashley. "Mom and Dad still there?"

"Yeah," said Jason. "I'll go with you."

As Ashley and Jason walked toward the back, Sofia was washing her car in front of the barn.

"When did you get home?" asked Jason.

"A minute ago," said Sofia.

"Can you wash my car too?" asked Ashley.

Sofia turned the hose toward her. Ashley shrieked and ran. Sofia laughed and sprayed Jason.

"Hey," cried Jason.

The sound of their parents laughing made Ashley turn. "What have you two been doing out here all week?" asked Ashley.

"We're stocking up the camper," said her mother. "My kids have huge appetite."

"Do you need any help?" asked Ashley.

"We're done for the day," said her father.

Jason wiped his face with his wet shirt. "Logan wants to go to church with us this Sunday."

"That's great," said her father.

"Should we take two cars?' asked Jason.

"Is Markus going as well?" asked her father.

"No," said Jason. "Only Logan."

Her father nodded. "Then, we'll fit in the SUV."

"I almost forgot about the SUV," said Ashley.

"It's your Dad's baby," said her mother.

"It's beautiful," said Ashley. "I'll see if Sofia needs help." She walked toward her sister. "Are you done?"

Sofia dried the windows with a large towel. "Almost."

Ashley wanted to approach Sofia regarding Logan, but she wasn't sure if it was the right move or even the right moment. Sofia was smiling and very happy. What if she and Jason were wrong? Perhaps they should step back and let God take over. Yes, she'd say a pray for Logan and Sofia if indeed Logan had feelings for her sister.

At the end, Ashley rolled up her sleeves. "Okay, what can I do to help you?"

Seven

Ashley smiled when Logan arrived on Sunday. He was taking Sunday best quite seriously. Because of his ironed blue dress shirt and jeans, Jason let out a sigh.

Jason ran fingers over his T-shirt. "Logan, you're making me look bad. I'll be back." He turned his heels and power-walked to his room. A few minutes later, he returned with a brown short-sleeve collared shirt.

"Wow, you're a great influencer, Logan," said Ashley.

Logan jumped back. Perhaps he didn't expect Ashley to make a joke. He smiled, exposing a pair of cute dimples. His face flushed. He ran his fingers through his neat straight hair.

Ashley found it pretty amusing, but she didn't want to make the poor guy uncomfortable. "I think we should leave now," she said.

"Yes, let's go," said her father.

They leapt into the SUV and her father drove away from the driveway. At the church, her father parked the SUV not far from the entrance. As they walked toward the church,

Logan kept glancing at the gift shop behind him.

"We're early," said Ashley. "Let's go to the gift shop."

"Yes, let's go," said Sofia.

Over the years, Ashley learned that her family loved the gift shop. They took pleasure in checking out every item. Some were the same items they saw week after week. No, they never grew tired of them. Logan stood in the middle of the shop and scanned his surroundings. Sofia approached him.

One thing Ashley admired about Sofia was her super friendliness. No wonder Logan liked her… if that was the case at all. Although Ashley had a sneaky feeling Logan liked her sister a lot! Feeling like a voyeur, she glanced away, but she heard their conversation.

"I'd like to buy a cross," said Logan.

"Come," said Sofia.

Ashley walked toward the books section. She picked up a booklet of Saints. Yes, she had one at home, but she could not get enough of them. Besides, there were a lot of saints out there. She wanted to know them all, if that was even a possibility.

"I'll wait for you outside," said Ashley's mother.

Ashley went to the counter to pay for the booklet of Saints. In front of her, Sofia and

Logan were paying for Logan's crucifix. Just as Logan took out his wallet, Sofia handed her money to the cashier.

"Hi Vanessa," said Sofia.

"Hey Sofia," said Vanessa. "Are you going to church or leaving?"

Sofia smiled. "I'm going."

The question wasn't a surprise to Ashley. Her whole family was well known for staying late and helping clean the church before going home after Mass.

"Thank you for buying the cross for me," said Logan.

"My pleasure," said Sofia. "It's the least I can do for making sure my laptop is in tip-top condition."

"Thank you so much." Logan held up his new cross to Vanessa. "This is my first cross."

Vanessa leaned forward. "It's a beautiful cross."

Ashley joined them at the counter and handed Vanessa the booklet and her credit card.

"This is a good one," said Vanessa. "Can add to your collection."

"You know me too well, it's scary," said Ashley.

After paying for her booklet, they said goodbye to Vanessa and went to the church.

"I'm a little nervous," said Logan. "I've never been to church."

"Don't worry," said Jason. "Just follow my lead."

"That's comforting," said Ashley.

Jason glanced over at her and made a face.

Ashley smiled and turned to Logan. "If you feel uncomfortable, you can either sit down or step outside."

Logan's eyes grew big. "Step outside?"

"Oh yes, people do it all the time," said Jason. "You'll see."

Sofia placed her hand on his shoulder. "Listen, I'll go with you. Just let me know."

Logan calmed down a little.

Ashley lifted her gaze upward. "*Well done, Sofia,"* she whispered. That was Sofia's gift – Eliminating people's fear and anxiety. Together, they entered the church.

"*Thank you, Lord,*" said Ashley to herself.

Eight

Sofia knelt and made the sign of the cross. After saying a short prayer, her mind wandered to Logan. There were talks in her family about Logan spending a lot of time in their house. They didn't mind it as they enjoyed his company. He was a polite and respectful young man. Sitting beside Logan, Sofia wondered why he wanted to go to church with them. She was exhilarated when she first heard about his intention, Through Markus, she knew his family practiced both Christianity and ancient animism. Perhaps, Logan could be the beacon his family needed. *Praise the Lord.*

After the Mass had ended, they hung out at the entrance of the church. Logan didn't step outside once. He even sang along, and he had a great voice. Sofia introduced Logan to all her friends. Ever so friendly, Logan was all smiles.

Her best friend, Melodie, whispered to her, "He's cute!"

To Sofia's surprise, blood rose to her cheeks. Her whole face was on fire, and she didn't know how to respond.

Ashley came to her rescue. "Hey Melodie," she said. "How are you?"

Melodie gave Ashley a big hug. "Hey Ashley! I miss you."

"Doing anything fun this summer?" asked Ashley.

Melodie released Ashley and shoved her hands in her jean's pocket. "I'm going to do some part time job at my uncle's, learning the ropes, no pun intended.

Melodie's uncle owned a boat shop at the marina. Sofia had seen the shop. There were a lot of ropes in there.

Ashley chuckled. "At least you get to enjoy the sun."

Melodie rubbed her hand over her arm. "Luckily, I need a tan."

They laughed.

"Good seeing you, Melodie," said Ashley. "Time for breakfast."

They bade farewell.

"Sofia!" Melodie called out.

Sofia turned.

Melodie held her thumb near her ear and her little finger pointed at her mouth, giving Sofia the "Call Me" sign.

Sofia nodded, waved, and walked away. Her father drove to the Mom and Pop restaurant not far from the church. After having her favorite breakfast skillet, they drove home.

* ~ | ~ | ~ * | * ~ | ~ | ~ *

Logan Spencer touched his new cross. Not only was the cross his very first, but it was bought by Sofia. Sitting next to her in church calmed the tornado inside him. The raging vortex subsided and quietened by Sofia's close presence. She looked so beautiful in her flowery summer dress. He wondered what the Flynns thought about him spending a lot of time with them. Even his own family questioned him. He simply said Jason needed his help. Yes, it wasn't the truth, but he couldn't state his true emotions. Not until he was certain of his own feelings. The one hour in the church, the minutes in the church's gift shop, and every second at the Flynn's home, he couldn't ignore nor deny his feelings any longer. He needed to act sooner before the Flynns took their month-long vacation.

"I'm going to the barn," said Sofia's father.

"I'll help you, Dad" said Jason. "Let me change first."

"I'll help too," said Ashley.

"What's your plan for the day?" asked Sofia.

Logan glanced down at his shirt.

Sofia smiled. "You should go home."

"I'd like to help," said Logan.

"You can wear my T-shirt," said Jason. He went into his room and returned with a blue T-shirt. "Here, try this. You can change in my room."

"I'm going to change too," said Sofia.

"Okay, see you out there," said Jason.

Logan changed his shirt and waited for Sofia. She came out with a tank top and shorts.

"You're beautiful..." As soon as those words came out of his mouth, he wished he could take it back.

Sofia's whole face reddened.

Logan ran his fingers through his hair. "I'm sorry, I shouldn't have said that."

Sofia smiled. "I... Well... Thank you."

They both let out a nervous chuckle.

"Are you ready for your vacation?" asked Logan.

"I think so," said Sofia.

"I'm going to miss... all of you," he said.

Sofia headed to the kitchen and filled up a cooler with bottles of water. "What are your family doing?"

Logan filled a cup with ice from the freezer and pour it in the cooler. "Makanda... My mom wants to go visit her family there."

"Ooh nice," said Sofia. "You can visit Giant City State Park."

Logan closed the lid to the cooler. "That's the plan. Have you been there?"

"Once," said Sofia. "I'd love to go back."

"You can come with us," said Logan.

Sofia smiled and lowered her head.

Logan felt like banging his head on the wall. "I'm sorry, I didn't mean to—"

Sofia tucked her hair behind her ear. "No, you're fine."

They stepped out of the house. Logan's heart began to race. If he wanted to sleep tonight, he'd better reveal his raging emotions that had kept him awake for the past week.

"Sofia," he whispered.

Sofia turned to him as she closed the door. "Yeah…"

The flutter in the pit of his stomach turned rampant. His mouth went dry. "I want to say… thank you for the cross."

Sofia gave him a big smile. "You're most welcome."

Together they walked toward the barn. Logan kept his head down. He wanted to kick himself that he couldn't bring himself to let Sofia know his true feelings.

Nine

Sofia thought she was going to die when Logan told her she was beautiful. Sure, she was flattered, but she was also petrified. For the past few days, she had been thinking about Logan. Yes, they spent a lot of time together. And yes, she would miss him when she went on vacation with her family. Deep within her heart, she wondered if there was something going on. Did Cupid play a trick on her? On both of them? She shook her head. No, she didn't want to be trapped in that wild maze.

At the barn, her family loaded the camper. They would leave early the next morning. Logan helped her mother loading the mini fridge.

"You want to come along?" her mother asked.

"I'd love to," said Logan. "But my family is leaving for Makanda next weekend."

"Ooh, Giant City State Park," said her father. "Nice place. How long are you going to be there?"

"A couple of weeks," said Logan.

"If you're bored next week, come visit us at Clinton Lake," said her father.

"I might come and visit," said Logan.

Sofia wasn't sure if that was a good or bad idea. Still, she smiled, silently hoping he would come before he headed down south. Sofia packed her tent and duffel bag in the back of her father's truck. Logan helped her.

After a few hours of loading stuff into the camper and truck, her father stood back and nodded. "We're all set," he said proudly. "We'll leave bright and early."

They walked out of the barn and her father closed the door.

Sofia leaned against her car. "I'm beat," she said.

Logan stood beside her, fanning himself. "It's hot in there."

"Yes, it is," said Sofia.

Her family headed inside.

"I should go," said Logan. "But I don't want to."

Sofia turned to him. His cheeks were red. *It could the heat in the barn*, she thought.

"I should get my shirt from Jason," he said and headed for the house.

Sofia waited until Logan was out of sight before making a call to her best friend.

"Hey, what's up?" said Melodie.

"Hey back," said Sofia.

"Wait, where is Logan?" asked Melodie.

Sofia shook her head. She had made the mistake of telling Melodie about Logan a couple of nights ago.

"He just went inside the house," said Sofia. "He helped us loading the camper."

"Wow, is he going with you guys?" asked Melodie.

"No, but my dad told him to visit if he's bored," said Sofia.

"I'm sure he'll come," said Melodie.

Sofia turned toward the house. No sign of Logan. "I think he likes me."

"YES!" cried Melodie.

Sofia moved the phone away from her ear. "Calm down. He didn't come out and say it, but he seemed like he wanted to tell me something. Melodie, I'm scared."

Melodie let out a sigh. "I know you don't want to get involved with anyone right now, but he seems nice and he's cute."

Sofia couldn't help but smiled. "I bought him a cross before Mass."

"That's wonderful," said Melodie.

"Not sure how his mom is going to take it," said Sofia.

"Why?" asked Melodie.

"His father is a Christian, but his mother practices animism and ancient rituals."

"How did you know?" asked Melodie.

"Jason is friends with Logan's brother."

"Oh yeah, you told me that," said Melodie. "Is that going to be a problem?"

"I don't know. We'll see." Sofia turned.

Logan came out and looked at her.

"Okay, got to go," said Sofia.

"Talk to you later," said Melodie.

Sofia ended the call and smiled at Logan. "Hey…"

Logan smiled and walked toward her. "I'm heading home."

Sofia shoved her phone in her pocket. "Are you going to visit us before you go down south?"

"I might," said Logan.

"You should," said Sofia.

Logan glanced at her as he stopped at his car. He looked around him. "Here goes," he whispered under his breath.

Sofia's eyes grew wide. "What?"

"Sofia, I… I'm going to miss you," he said.

Sofia took a deep breath. "*It's now or never*," she told herself. "I'm going to miss you too, Logan."

There was a shining glow in Logan's eyes. "Really?"

Sofia nodded.

Logan's chest rose. "I really like you."

Sofia froze.

"I'm sorry," said Logan. "I…"

As much as Sofia wanted Logan to finish his words, she couldn't watch him fumbling. She cleared her throat. "I like you too," she confessed.

They stood still like statues. Their eyes locked.

A squirrel ran past them. That seemed to snap them out of a deep spell.

Logan unlocked his car. "I'll see you soon," he said.

Sofia couldn't find her voice. She simply nodded and waved.

Ten

Logan started his car with much trembling hand. His fingers shook so bad. He reversed his car and stopped for a second. He waved and drove away. From his rearview mirror, he could see Sofia standing at her driveway.

"I did it," he cried out loud. "Omigosh, I told her. I told Sofia I like her."

He smiled his whole way home. His eyes caught the sight of an old yew tree on the edge of his family farm. He drove toward the tree and stopped the car. Growing up, he loved the tree. Every chance he got he would play in the tree hollow. He stepped into the tree hollow and sat down.

"Hello Old Friend," he whispered.

He looked up. It was a little dark. "I met a girl. Her name is Sofia Flynn. I like her and I told her. I hope I did the right thing."

He knew his father would accept this relationship. His mother, on the other hand… His heart saddened. He touched the inside of the trunk with one hand. He wrapped his other hand around the cross Sofia bought for him.

"Give me strength," he begged.

After a few minutes, he crawled out. Again, he touched the tree. "I love you, Old Friend."

He got back into his car and called his brother.

"Hey Logan," said Markus.

"Hey, where are you?" asked Logan.

"On my way home," said Markus. "Are you still at Jason's?"

Logan's face felt warm. "No, I'm at the farm."

"What are you doing there?" asked Markus.

Logan looked up at the tree. "I just stopped by the yew tree."

"Oh man, I forgot…"

Logan chuckled. "You better stop by when you can."

"Wait for me," said Markus. "I'll be there in a few."

"All right." Logan ended the call and breathed in the fresh air. "It's good to be home."

While waiting for his brother, he cleaned the cavity in the bole of his favorite tree. Just as he was finishing up, Markus pulled up behind his car.

"Hey bro." Markus stepped out of his car.

Logan rubbed his hands together. "You came at the right time."

Markus laughed. "I'm good at that." He glanced inside the hollow of the tree. "Wow, you did a great job."

"I'm tempted to spend the night out here," said Logan.

"We used to do that," said Markus.

"Yeah, we did," said Logan.

Markus picked up a stick and threw it across the field. "Are you ready for Makanda?"

"Sure, how about you?" asked Logan.

Markus planted both of his fists on his sides. "Hmm…"

Logan narrowed his brows. "What's wrong?"

"Laurel wants me to go hiking with her," said Markus.

"When?" asked Logan.

Markus picked up another stick and snapped it into two. "Next week."

"Ouch," Logan said.

Markus leaned against Logan's car. "Mom doesn't seem too fond of Laurel."

"What?" Logan was feeling exasperated. He wanted to scream. "Mom hasn't even met her yet."

Markus gave him the look that said, "*Are you serious?*"

Logan nodded. His mother knew this thing. His mind wandered to The Room.

"I plan for them to meet in the next day or so," said Markus. "I don't want to lose Laurel, Logan."

Logan's heart went out to his brother. "Spend more time at home. Maybe that'll change her mind a bit."

"Yeah, that's what I thought too," said Markus.

Logan scratched his temple. "Then again, don't listen to me. I haven't been home much either."

Markus tried to smile. "Where were you?"

"At Jason's."

"What are you doing there?" asked Markus. "I know you like the barn and all."

Logan turned to the yew tree. He touched his cross. "Do you know Jason's family well?"

"Of course," said Markus. "I've known Jason for years."

"What do you think of Sofia?" asked Logan.

Markus stood in front of him and tilted his head. "Why... Wait, you..." He pointed at Logan.

Logan rubbed his hand on the cross. "I like Sofia Flynn."

Markus scratched his head. "Wow, I didn't see that coming."

"She's amazing," said Logan.

Markus narrowed his brows at him. "Amazing?"

"It's not what you think," said Logan. "She's a wonderful person. She's very friendly and nice."

Markus nodded. "That's true," he said. "Does she know?"

"I've just told her that I like her."

"Wow," said Markus. "Does Jason know?"

Logan shook his head. "Although I think he suspected it."

Markus smiled. "I won't be surprised if he does." He wrapped his arm around Logan's shoulder. "Wow, this is great news, bro. I'm so happy for you."

Logan felt good. "I really like her."

"Please don't break her heart," said Markus. "Jason will kill you."

Logan laughed. "Not a chance. She's perfect."

Markus eyed his cross. "Where did you get that?"

Logan held up his cross. "Don't freak out. I went to church this morning and Sofia bought this cross for me."

Markus rubbed his chin. "At least you'll have Dad's blessing."

"I'm worried about Mom," said Logan.

"You have one good thing going for you," said Markus. "Mom knows the Flynns and she likes them."

Logan's thoughts went to Holly, his first and only girlfriend before he met Sofia. "I hate to say this… Do you think Mom had anything to do with Holly breaking up with me?"

Markus let out a loud sigh. "Could be… That's why I'm scared of Laurel meeting Mom."

"Our family is so messed up," said Logan.

Markus's phone beeped. He pulled it out from his pocket. "It's Mom." He pressed the green button. "Hi Mom… I'm with Logan out in the field… We're cleaning out the Yew tree." Markus smiled and gave Logan a thumb up. "Yeah, we missed the old tree, Mom…" His smile grew wider. "Yeah, we're almost done. We'll come home soon." He ended the call. "I think we're on Mom's good side right now."

"That's awesome," said Logan. "Let's go home."

Markus nodded. They got into their own cars and drove away.

Logan turned back. "I'll come back soon, Old Friend."

Eleven

Logan called Sofia the next morning. They texted all day. He and Markus stayed home the whole day. Markus didn't even touch his phone in front of his mother. Yes, he was trying to get on his mother's good side. That night, Markus entered his room and plopped down on the edge of Logan's bed.

"I'm going to bring Laurel to see Mom tomorrow," said Markus.

"Bring her to the Yew tree first," said Logan.

Markus snapped her fingers. "Good idea."

"Have you told Mom yet?" asked Logan.

"Tomorrow morning," said Markus.

"Good luck, bro," said Logan.

"You'll be here right?" asked Markus.

"Of course," said Logan.

"Are you going to see Sofia before the weekend?" asked Markus.

"I'm planning on it," said Logan.

"You know what, bring Sofia over tomorrow," said Markus.

"Very funny," said Logan.

Markus scooted toward his brother. "Listen, you should ask Sofia. You wouldn't be too petrified when you bring Sofia home by YOURSELF later on."

Logan's heart raced like the "L" in downtown Chicago. "You've got a point." He stared at his phone.

"Text Sofia," begged Markus.

The idea of Sofia meeting his Mom scared him to death. Just the thought of it gave him a killer migraine. Logan pressed the Message icon. He stared at the screen, unsure of what to say.

"Tell her Markus is bringing his girlfriend home for the first time. He asked if you'd like to come along."

Logan thought for a second and thought it didn't sound so bad. He nodded and typed. His index finger shook as it hovered above the Send button. Markus leaned over and pressed the Send button.

Logan watched in horror. He and Markus stared at the screen. There was no reply.

"Omigosh, I'm doomed," said Logan.

"She might be sleeping," said Markus.

That soothed him a little. They did say good night an hour ago.

"Don't worry, I'll talk to Sofia tomorrow," said Markus as he bade goodnight and left him in the dark.

Logan tossed and turned for hours before falling asleep.

The next morning, every inch of Logan's body ached. He jumped and looked around the bed for his phone. Then, he caught sight of his phone, charging on the end table. There was a notification that he had unread messages. He quickly removed the charging cable and unlocked his phone.

It was a message from Sofia. "*Good morning, I'm sorry I didn't see your message last night. I went to sleep and put my phone on silent.*" A few seconds later, another message from Sofia. "*It's funny, I wanted to ask you if you could drive me home to pick up some stuff. I'd love to stop by your house for a few minutes. Tell Markus he owes me one.*"

Logan smiled. "Thank you, Lord," he whispered. He typed, "*Good morning. You made my day. What time do you want me to pick you up?*"

Sofia replied, "*How about after lunch?*"

Logan texted back, "*Sounds good. I'll see you soon.*" He got out of his room and raced into Markus's room.

Markus jumped. "You scared me!"

"Sorry," said Logan. He approached his brother. "Sofia said you owe her big time."

Markus sat up. "Seriously, she'll come?"

"We're lucky," said Logan. "She wants to pick up some stuff from her house."

Markus grabbed his phone from his end table. "Perfect," he said as he typed something in his phone.

Logan walked toward the window and peeked outside. He could see the farm, but not the Yew tree.

"Yes!" cried Markus.

Logan turned.

"She said yes," said Markus.

"Awesome," said Logan. "We better tell Mom, but how?"

"We'll think of something." Markus leapt from his bed and headed for the bathroom.

Logan plopped down on Markus's bed. His mind was racing. At that moment, his phone beeped.

There was a message from Sofia. "*Hey, can Jason come along?*"

Logan's heart ballooned. "Perfect," he said. He typed, "*Of course. See you two soon.*"

When Markus stepped out, Logan straightened. "Guess what, I just received a text from Sofia that Jason wants to come along."

Markus's face brightened. "This is perfect."

"That's exactly what I said," said Logan. "I'll tell Mom I'm going to give a ride to Jason and Sofia and they'll stop by for a few minutes."

"And I'll chime in and say I'll bring Laurel as well," said Markus. "When you leave, I can leave too."

"This is it," said Logan.

Markus raised his hand and they high-fived each other. "Let's go."

They both walked out of Markus's room into the kitchen. His mother was fixing breakfast.

"Good morning, Mom," said Logan, followed by Markus.

"Good morning," said their mother.

They sat down. "Jason and his family are in Clinton," said Logan.

"Aah, they go camping every year," said his mother.

"Yeah," said Logan. "I'm going there later."

His mother turned to him. In her hand was a skillet full of bacon grease.

A huge lump appeared in Logan's throat. "Jason and his sister want to pick up some stuff from their house."

"That's one thing I don't like about camping," said his mother. "We always forget something."

"Yeah," said Logan. "They want to see the Yew tree. We'll come by here after."

His mother handed the bacon to Markus. "That's wonderful. I haven't seen Jason for a while."

Markus took a bite of the bacon. "You know what, I'll bring Laurel here as well. You haven't met her yet, Mom."

His mother lowered her head and eyed Markus. Logan's heart stopped beating.

After a few second, she nodded. "I'd like to meet her," she said.

Logan exhaled under his breath. His father entered the kitchen and saved them all from a very awkward and terrifying moment.

Twelve

Sofia stood in front of the Yew tree. The hole in the trunk mesmerized her. "Wow," she said.

"You can go inside," said Logan.

Without thinking twice, Sofia crawled inside and sat up. "Wow," again she said. "This is amazing." She ran her fingers along inside of the tree.

Logan joined her. "She's my Old Friend. I spent a lot of time here when I was a kid."

"I would too," she said. "You're lucky."

Logan placed both his hands on the sacred ground. Slowly, he raised one of his hands to his cross. "Thank you," he said.

"For what?" asked Sofia.

Logan removed his hand from the cross, but not before Sofia noticed it. "For being here."

"I love it," she said.

"Okay, our turn," said Markus from outside the tree.

Sofia laughed. "Oops."

Sofia and Logan crawled out. Markus and Laurel went inside the hollow of the tree. Sofia looked around. Jason was climbing an Oak tree not far from them.

"He always climbs that tree whenever he's here," said Logan.

Sofia knew her brother was close to Markus, but she didn't realize he spent a lot of time out here. She glanced over her shoulder at the Yew tree. "I really like that tree."

"Me too," said Logan.

After a few minutes, Markus and Laurel joined them. Markus leaned toward Sofia. "Thank you for coming," he whispered.

"My pleasure," Sofia whispered back.

Markus turned toward the Oak tree. "Hey Jason, let's go!"

Jason waved and climbed down.

"He's obsessed with that tree," said Markus.

"It's magnificent," said Laurel. Her long blond hair flew in the wind. She smiled.

"*She has a beautiful smile*," thought Sofia. "*No wonder Markus fell for her.*"

Jason raced toward them. "Okay, I'm ready. I love that oak tree."

"Oh, we know," said Logan.

They all laughed. After a few minutes, they arrived at Logan's parent's home.

Jason got out and raced up the stairs. "Arlette! Basil!" he cried out. "I'm here!"

The door flew open. The older stood by the door with huge smiles.

"My parents," said Markus.

"Jason, it's been a long time," said Basil.

"Come in, Jason," said Arlette.

Jason rushed inside.

Arlette stood on top of the stairs. She stared at Laurel before studying her. Sofia's heart went amok.

"Okay, I'm petrified," Sofia whispered to Logan.

"Don't worry, I won't leave your side," said Logan.

"Okay, shall we?" asked Markus.

Together they walked up the stairs.

"Mom, Dad, this is Laurel," said Markus.

Logan turned to Sofia.

Thankfully, Jason reappeared. "That's my sister, Sofia," he said.

Arlette's face lit up. "Ah, welcome, Sofia."

Markus held Laurel's hand.

Sofia felt guilty. "Hi," she said. "I'm Sofia."

"I'm Arlette, Markus's mother," said Arlette. She turned to Basil.

"And I'm Basil, Markus's father," said Basil.

"Hi," said Sofia.

"Hello," said Laurel.

Basil gave Laurel a hug. "Welcome." Then, he gave Sofia a hug as well. "Come in."

Sofia sat down next to Jason. Arlette brought out some drinks and after sitting down with them for a few seconds, she excused herself. Logan exchanged glances with Markus. Sofia wondered what that was all about. Basil hadn't skipped a bit. He talked about the farm and their upcoming trip to Makanda. He sounded so excited.

Sofia heard a door creak. Again, Logan and Basil exchanged glances. Jason didn't seem to notice or care.

"Can I use the bathroom before we leave?" asked Sofia.

"Sure," said Logan. "I'll show you."

Logan led Sofia along the hallway. Sofia heard some weird noise as they walked past a room. She turned to Logan.

Logan simply smiled and opened the door to the bathroom. "Here you go."

"Thank you," said Sofia.

As she headed back to join the others, the back room was open. She glanced inside. The first thing she saw was a wall-mounted shelf with a small gold jar. Urn was the first word that came to mind.

"*Must be a family member's ashes*," thought Sofia. Instinctively, she made the sign of the cross. "*May your soul rest in peace*."

In the living room, Arlette was sitting next to Basil. Her gaze fluttered from Laurel to her. There was a strange look on her face. Sweat beaded on Sofia's scalp.

"Are you ready?" asked Jason.

Sofia nodded. "It's really nice meeting you, Arlette… Basil."

Basil stood. "Same here. Come again."

Jason hugged Basil. When he approached Arlette, she gave him the biggest smile Sofia had ever seen and hugged him. She really liked her brother.

"I'll come again soon. I promise," said Jason.

"You better," said Arlette. When she turned to Sofia and gave her a tight hug, a huge burden was lifted off her shoulder. "It's great meeting you, Sofia."

"We should go too," said Markus.

Arlette and Basil gave Laurel a quick hug. Again, Sofia felt guilty. They hurried out the door. Sofia did not breathe again until she got into the backseat of Logan's car. She wanted to ask what was in the room, but decided to let it rest.

Thirteen

After a month long of camping, Ashley and her family packed up and left. As much as she enjoyed the nature, she was happy to be home. She missed the comfort of her room.

"Welcome home," said Ashley, as her father parked the RV in the barn.

"Don't sound too excited," teased Sofia.

"Come one, you're happy to be home as well," said Ashley.

Sofia chuckled. "I'm just not too vocal about it."

Jason grabbed the cooler.

"We'll unload tomorrow," said her father. "Let's go inside."

Ashley snorted. "See, Dad is glad to be home."

"Don't tell your mother," her father whispered.

"I heard that," said her mother.

Ashley smiled and walked out of the barn. She got into the shower. The hot water felt good. After a few minutes, she had to step out. With a sigh, she turned off the faucet and returned into her room. She stood in front of the altar and lit the candle.

"Thank you for keeping us safe, Lord." She sat down on her bed and leaned her head back. She pulled out her Rosary from her purse and prayed. "Thank you, Mother Mary."

That night, Logan stopped by. Ashley stayed in her room until she completed all four mysteries of the Rosary. Once she had done praying, she rolled out of bed and blew out the candle on the altar.

She stepped out of her room. She heard laughter in the kitchen. Just as she headed toward the sound, something stirred inside her, as if saying, "*Be on guard, Ashley.*"

She turned her head slightly toward the hallway that led to the living room.

Her gaze landed on a pair of very tanned feet stopped at the end of the hallway. Right above the ankle was something white. She blinked. The feet disappeared. Believing her eyes were playing tricks on her, she shook her head, and entered the kitchen. She stopped and narrowed her eyes on the floor. It looked like a cross.

"What is that?" she asked.

"What?" asked Jason.

Ashley pointed to the floor by Logan's chair.

"Is that your cross, Logan?" asked Jason.

Logan touched his neck and looked around. The chain was on his lap. Jason picked up the cross and handed it to Logan.

"Thank you," said Logan. He checked the metal bail around the cross. It was closed shut. He fed the chain through the bail and wore it around his neck.

Jason handed her a slice of pizza. "Have some, Ashley."

"Thanks," Ashley pulled out a chair and sat down.

Ashley joined them until Logan left just before midnight. She was ready to sleep when someone knocked at her door. She opened it. Jason entered and scratched his head.

"What's on your mind, Jason?" asked Ashley.

Jason sat down on the edge of her bed. "There's no doubt Logan likes Sofia."

Ashley yawned and her mouth hung open. "Well, we kinda suspected that. How did you know?"

"Logan told me," he said.

"Well, Logan is a nice guy," said Ashley.

"It's not Logan that I'm worried about," said Jason.

"Logan's family?" asked Ashley.

"Yeah," said Jason. "Markus thought his mother had something to do with Logan's first girlfriend breaking up with him."

"Why?" asked Ashley.

Jason shrugged. "You know Markus's mother is an animist."

"They still celebrate Christmas," said Ashley.

"Who doesn't?" asked Jason. "It's a day to get free gifts."

Ashley chuckled. "Good point."

"Logan's ex is a devout Christian," said Jason. "She'll never allow Logan to be anything but…"

"The Spencers are nice folks," said Ashley.

"Perhaps my thoughts are spiraling out of control," said Jason.

"We'll pray," said Ashley.

"Yes, we shall," said Jason. "Good night."

Jason left the room. Ashley pulled out her Rosary. It was time for another round of prayers. She prayed until she fell asleep. When she woke up, her fingers were still clasping her Rosary.

Fourteen

Ashley thought of what Jason said the night before. As much as she liked Logan and his family, she loved Sofia first. She wanted to talk to Sofia, but decided to wait for Sofia to approach her. Her wish came true when Sofia entered her room after one knock.

"Good that you're up," said Sofia.

"What's up?" asked Ashley.

"Do you have a sec?" asked Sofia.

Ashley eyed the candle flickering on the altar. "Sure."

"What do you think about Logan?" asked Sofia.

Ashley eyed her sister. She looked serious. Ashley decided not to tease her. "He seems nice. Why?"

Sofia plopped down on her bed and wrapped her arms around her pillow. "He told me he liked me."

"Wow, what did you say?" asked Ashley.

"I told him I… I like him too," said Sofia.

Ashley nodded her head slowly and sat next to her sister. "He's a nice guy, Sofia. His family is nice too."

"So, you approve?" asked Sofia.

Ashley smiled. "You have my blessing."

Sofia leaned forward and hugged her. "Thank you, Sis." Sofia released her and went on, "You know Jason and I went to see his parents."

"Oh yeah, how did that go?" asked Ashley.

"It was scary," said Sofia. "I'm glad Jason went with me. I feel sorry for Laurel, Markus's girlfriend."

"It's always scary to meet your future in-law," said Ashley.

Sofia took the pillow and threw it at her. Ashley laughed.

"Let's get breakfast," said Sofia.

Together, they went to the kitchen and joined their parents. Jason didn't wake up until they were done eating.

That evening, Logan stopped by. Ashley accepted him as a part of her family. From the looks of her parents' face, they did too. Again, Ashley stayed in her room. She said her Rosary and blew the candle. She made the sign of the cross and walked out of her room.

Ashley turned into the hallway to the living room. Logan was lying down on the sofa. Sofia sat on the recliner next to him. As Ashley entered the living room, something moved inside her. The same sensation as the night before. She turned to the door. The back of a pair of tanned feet with no shoes were heading toward the front door. In an instant, the prayer to Saint Michael the Archangel burst from her lips in silent. She moved her gaze upward. As soon as she saw the white above the ankle, the feet disappeared.

"*This can't be a coincidence*," she said to herself.

Almost in an instant, Ashley asked, "Logan, where's your cross?"

Logan touched his neck. This time, the chain slipped to the floor. Next to his chain was his cross. "How did you know?"

Ashley entered the living room and glanced up at the clock. It was around 9 P.M. She didn't like talking about weird stuff at night. But this needed to be addressed. *This is her home*. She wouldn't allow anything or anyone violated the safety of her home.

Logan leapt to his feet. He picked up his chain and cross from the floor. Once the chain was safely around his neck, he turned to Ashley.

Before Ashley said a word, she whispered, "*Be with us, Lord Jesus*." She took a deep breath. "I saw something."

"Saw what?" asked Jason.

Ashley turned to her parents. They looked at her. Their intense gaze spoke volumes. She needed to proceed with caution.

Sofia straightened. "Ashley, what did you see?"

Ashley sat down. "I saw a pair of feet walking toward the front door."

"Close the door," shrieked Sofia.

Logan's face turned white.

Jason got up and locked the door. "What else did you see?"

"I only saw a pair of tanned feet and above the ankle was something white," said Ashley. "Like a choir robe."

"Did you see the face?" asked Jason.

Ashley shook her head. Again, she eyed the clock. Five minutes had passed. She went on, "Last night, I saw the same feet by the hallway toward the kitchen."

Sofia spun toward her. "Why didn't you say something?"

"It was late," said Ashley. "I thought my eyes were playing tricks on me."

"It is late," said her father. "We should call it a night. Logan, tell your parents you're spending the night here." He got up and went to his room.

His mother followed suit. "Go to sleep early and say your prayers."

"I'm sorry," said Ashley.

"No, thank you for telling me," said Logan. He eyed the door.

"You're staying, Logan," said Jason. "You can sleep in my room."

Sofia stood. "No, you can sleep in my room."

Ashley and Jason froze.

"Aah…" Logan didn't finish.

Sofia's face turned red. "It's nothing like that… I'm going to sleep in Ashley's room."

Ashley smiled. "Let's go to sleep, guys."

When Sofia entered Ashley's room, she was shaking. "What's going on, Ashley?"

"Shh… Let's not talk about it now," said Ashley.

"I'm scared," she said. "Can we have the lights on?"

"Of course," said Ashley. "Let's say the prayer to our Guardian Angel together."

Sofia nodded and together they said the prayer in unison.

Ashley clasped her Rosary in her hand.

Fifteen

The next morning, Ashley opened her eyes. She couldn't find her Rosary. She turned. Sofia was holding it. Ashley smiled and got up. When she returned, Sofia was on her feet, stretching.

"Thank you for letting me sleep in here," said Sofia.

"I'm grateful for the company," said Ashley.

Sofia rubbed her arms. "I'm scared, Ashley. Why did this happen?"

"I don't know," said Ashley. "We'll pray about it."

Sofia touched her throat. "I prayed the Rosary until my throat went dry."

Ashley smiled. "Come on, let's get some breakfast."

In the kitchen, her parents were eating with Logan. To Ashley's great surprise, Jason was also up. They exchanged their usual 'Morning' greeting.

"I'll go change and join you in a bit," said Sofia as hurried into her room.

Ashley sat down.

"I'm sorry about last night," said Logan. "I don't know what's happening."

"It's not your fault," said Ashley.

"So, you saw this person two times?" asked her mother.

"I only saw the feet and a little bit of white robe before the feet disappeared," said Ashley. She turned to the hallway and looked away.

"Bare feet?" asked Logan.

Ashley nodded.

"Could be nothing," said her father. "Maybe it's just being curious."

"We'll pray about it," said her mother.

Ashley nodded.

Sofia joined them and plopped down beside Logan.

Without looking at Sofia, Logan said, "I'll stop coming if that's what you all want."

Sofia faced him, but nothing came out from her.

"Don't be silly," said Ashley. "You're a part of the family."

Logan's face immediately reddened.

Ashley went on. "You can come anytime you want."

"Ashley's right," said her father. "You don't have to stop coming."

Jason nodded. "Agreed."

"You're welcome here any time, Logan," said her mother.

Sofia was the only one that was still quiet.

~|~|~|*~|~|~*

Logan had never felt so guilty in his life. What exactly did Ashley see? The look Sofia gave her jabbed his heart like a sharp dagger. Her silence sliced his soul even deeper. After breakfast, Ashley left the kitchen with her parents. Jason left a few minutes later after placing his hand on his shoulder.

"Sofia..." Logan stopped.

"I'm scared," said Sofia.

"I don't know what's going on," he said. "But I'll get to the bottom of it. Please don't give up on me."

Sofia faced him. To his surprise, she touched his cheek. "I'm not giving up on you. I just want to know what's going on."

"I'll head home and ask my mother," he said.

Sofia's eyes widened.

He grabbed her hands. "If anyone can give me an answer, it's her."

Sofia nodded. "You'll come back tonight?"

"I'll be here," he said.

"Okay," she said.

Logan helped her with the dishes.

"No, I got it," she said.

Logan took that as a hint to go. "I'll see you soon." He leaned toward her and kissed the top of her head.

Before Sofia could react, he left the kitchen. He bade goodbye to the family and returned home. He stopped at the Yew tree first.

He sat down on the root. "I need help, Old Friend. Is it the family's Guardian?" He entered the hole and sat down. After his whole body calmed down, he said goodbye and drove home. He parked his car beside Markus's. His father was working on his old truck outside the garage.

"Hey Dad," said Logan.

"Hey, how's Jason?" he asked.

Logan smiled. "He's fine, Dad."

His father leaned back and faced Logan. "Are you okay?"

Logan turned to the house. "Something happened at Jason's last night."

His father looked at the house as well. "What are you talking about?"

"Ashley… Jason's sister, saw a pair of bare feet in the house."

His father froze.

"Twice, Dad," said Logan. His voice cracked. "Was it, Mom?"

His father rubbed his face. "Omigosh. Is everyone all right?"

"I hope so," said Logan.

His father's chest rose and fell. "Let's go talk to your mother. She's gone too far."

"Mom!" Logan called out. "Mom!"

His mother stepped out from The Room. "What is it? Why are you screaming?"

Markus peered at him from the kitchen. He was chewing something.

"What happened last night?" asked Logan.

Markus's mouth hung open.

"What are you talking about?" his mother asked.

"You sent the Guardian to Jason's home?" his father yelled. "Are you out of your mind?"

Markus froze in the hallway.

His mother opened her mouth and closed it again. "How…"

"Ashley saw her feet, Mom," said Logan.

His mother eyed the cross hanging around his neck.

Logan touched his cross. "Sofia gave this to me. I will never take it off." His voice shook as he continued, "Never, Mom."

"This has to stop, Arlette," said his father.

His mother turned to Markus. He returned to the kitchen. His mother let out a heavy sigh and left the living room. She returned to The Room and slammed the door.

Markus ran out the kitchen and joined Logan. "I'm sorry this happened," he said.

"Me too," said Logan. "If anything happens to the Flynns, I'll never forgive myself."

Sixteen

For a whole week, Ashley did not see anything strange lurking in the house. Logan and Sofia were closer than ever. Her parents knew about their relationship before Logan and Sofia told them. Her parents accepted Logan the moment he entered their home.

"*Well, that's my parents*," thought Ashley. "*Ever so loving toward fellow human being and animals alike*." Her parents would feed the stray dogs and cats and of course the birds, especially in the winter. Their favorite are the non-migratory cardinals. *Who doesn't love the Cardinals*? Ashley smiled.

That Sunday night, Ashley left the coziness of her room. Logan was hanging out with Jason and Sofia on the front porch. The front door was wide open. Something nudged at her heart. The strange flutters returned.

"*No*," she said to herself.

As she looked at Logan, a pair of feet by the door caught her eye. Again, her lips mumbled the prayer to Saint Michael the Archangel. At the same time, she glanced upward. The white robe came into view. She looked up higher. More white. Again, her gaze moved up until a face appeared. It was a tanned oval face of a woman with long silver hair. The woman froze. Her tanned hand was on the door jamb. Their eyes locked. Her silver eyes widened. The corner of her lip curled up ever so slightly.

After a few seconds of some sort of staring contest, the woman gave Ashley a tiny nod. Then, her face faded. Within seconds, the woman vanished into thin air. Ashley took a deep breath. She blinked. The woman was no longer there.

Ashley glanced at Logan and her siblings. They looked so happy. She didn't want to ruin the joyful evening. Yet, she didn't want them sitting out there.

"Hey guys, can all of you come inside?" asked Ashley.

Jason turned to her. "Why?"

"Come inside please," said Ashley. "Wait, Logan, do you still have your cross?"

Sofia let out a yelp and dashed inside. She raced to stand behind Ashley. Her parents leaned forward and looked at each other.

"You saw the feet again?" asked her father.

Ashley simply nodded. She hadn't moved an inch. She kept looking at the door. The woman was at the doorstep a moment ago. She didn't want the woman to come inside.

Logan touched his neck. The chain was hanging around his neck but there was no cross.

He let out a string of curses. "Stop coming here!" he screamed. "I'll never stop wearing the cross."

Ashley scanned the living room. Her heart hammered. No sign of the mysterious woman.

Jason found Logan's cross next to his chair and picked it up. Together, they scurried inside the living room. Jason locked the door.

Logan grabbed his phone and tapped the screen with his fingers.

"What are you doing?" asked Ashley.

"My mother has to stop," said Logan. "This has gone too far." His voice shook.

"Put your phone down, Logan," said Ashley.

Sofia faced her. Ashley shook her head.

"We say things we don't mean when we're upset," said Ashley.

After being so quiet, her mother said, "Ashley's right. You can talk to your mother in the morning."

Ashley opened her mouth to speak. Something stirred in Ashley's heart. She decided she would not mention the woman's face. No reason to scare her family this late of the night.

Logan's phone rang. He jumped. Everyone in the room looked at him. Ashley's mother's lips were moving.

Ashley joined her mother and said the Lord's Prayer.

Seventeen

Logan glanced at the Caller ID. It was his brother. "Hello," he whispered.

"Hey, are you at Jason's?" asked Markus.

Logan wrinkled his brows. He could hear Markus's deep breathing. Markus inhaled and exhaled loudly.

"Yeah," said Logan.

"I'll stop by and pick you up," said Markus.

Logan jerked his head back. "Are you okay?"

Markus let out a loud sigh. "We'll talk soon." He ended the call.

Logan stared at his phone until the screen went dark. He cleared his throat. "Markus is coming to pick me up."

Sofia touched his trembling hand. "Is he okay?"

"I'm not sure," said Logan. "Markus didn't sound his usual self."

Jason turned to Ashley. If Logan had to guess, he bet they were thinking about the mysterious feet. The hair on his arms stood straight up. What if something happened to Laurel? His mother must stop this madness. He'd destroy the jar in The Room!

The sound of wheels screeching to a stop made Logan leap to his feet. Sofia's parents peered out the window. The motion light came on. Markus stepped out of his car.

Jason opened the door. "Hey Markus."

"Hey Jason," said Markus.

Logan appeared behind Jason. "I'll be right there."

"Do you want to come inside?" asked Jason.

"Can I take a rain check?" asked Markus.

"Sure," said Jason.

Logan faced Sofia. "I'm sorry… I have to go."

"Be careful out there," said Sofia's mother.

Logan faked a smile. "I will." He looked at everyone in the living room. "See you all tomorrow." His eyes burned. "Again, I'm really sorry for what happened."

Before he lost it, Logan ran down the stairs into Markus's car.

Markus waved at Jason. "Bye."

Jason waved back.

Logan leaned back in the seat as Markus reversed and drove away.

"I'm sorry for stopping by like this," said Markus.

"What's going on?" asked Logan.

Markus scratched his temple. "Laurel and I went to the mall and we saw Holly."

Logan felt like Markus had just punched him in the gut. Here he thought something happened to Laurel and Markus. "You called me because of Holly?"

"This is serious," said Markus.

That got Logan's attention. "Spill it out."

"Do you know why Holly broke up with you?" asked Markus.

The feet Ashley mentioned came back to haunt him. "I can't believe this."

Markus let out a sigh and faced him. "It's our mother, Logan."

Logan wanted to throw up. He rolled down the window and stuck his head out. He inhaled the night air before pulling his head back inside. "Why were you talking about me? Do you do this a lot?"

Markus let out another sigh. "It's nothing like that. Holly was staring at me. Laurel asked who she was."

That calmed Logan a little.

"So, I introduced Laurel to Holly," said Markus.

Logan nodded. "And…"

Markus focused on the road. "She asked how you were."

Logan held his breath.

"I told her you're going out with Jason's sister," said Markus.

Logan scratched a fake itch on his ear. "Why did you say that?"

Markus glared at him. "Why not?" He snorted. "She dumped you."

Ouch! That hurts, thought Logan.

"It was then she told us what really happened." Markus grabbed the steering wheel with both hands. "Mom told Holly to stop seeing you. OUR mother paid her $25,000 to dump you."

Logan's eyes burned. "Wh... What?" His whole body was on fire. "Did she take the money?"

Markus slowly nodded. "I'm sorry, Logan."

The old wound ripped open. "I can't believe this. She left me for a measly twenty-five grand."

"That's what I said too," said Markus. "But her explanation made all the sense in the world."

"And what's that?" asked Logan.

"Put yourself in her shoes," said Markus. "Would you want to be with a family that didn't want you?"

Logan didn't answer.

Markus went on. "Yes, she lo... loved you, but she couldn't face our mother, Logan. I hate to say this, I agree with her."

Logan looked out the window. The cold night wind made his eyes tear.

Eighteen

Logan watched the stars surround the moon in the dark sky. At the Flynns' home, he was surrounded by love. Sofia's whole family loved him. And he loved them back. No ifs or buts about it. Now, Markus had to bring up Holly. She was his first girlfriend from high school. He gave her his heart. There was no doubt Holly still owned a piece of him. His throat burned. His heart flattened. The moon hid behind the dark clouds to give him much needed privacy. Logan wondered if he was hiding his true feelings for Holly too.

"*Do I still love Holly*?" he interrogated himself. Before he could answer, Sofia's smiling face flashed before his eyes. "I love Sofia," he whispered.

"That's good," said Markus.

Logan spun toward his brother. "I'm torn, Markus."

"You were broken," said Markus. "No, I take that back. You were blown to pieces."

Although it sounded like Markus was exaggerating, his words were very close to the truth.

Markus went on. "Remember who put you back together again."

Logan knew Markus meant Sofia. Although he hated to admit defeat, his brother was right. "I think you're afraid of Jason."

Markus grinned. "I love the Flynns. And I like Sofia very much."

Logan nodded. "I don't know if I should reach out to Holly."

"Do you want to open the pandora box?" asked Markus.

Logan's chest felt crushed. A very familiar pain oozed from every inch of his body. "I owe her an apology."

"I wouldn't suggest it," said Markus.

The sky lit up. The moon was visible once more. Yes, he was in the darkness for one torturous year. Sofia was the light that brought him out of his ominous tunnel. A part of him was scared to see Holly. What if he fell for her all over again? No, he couldn't hurt Sofia. He promised Sofia and himself not to break her heart.

Logan stared at the moon. "You're right. It's time to end this chapter of my life." Why did the pain still linger on? It was excruciating. He bit the inside of his cheek until he tasted blood. "Mom needs to stop interfering with my life!"

"Laurel's scared of her, Logan," said Markus. "I don't want to lose Laurel." His voice cracked.

Before they reached the ramp to the freeway, Markus made a U-turn. "Do you want to go back to Jason's?"

"No," said Logan. "There's something I want to tell you."

"What is it?" asked Markus.

"I think Ashley saw the Guardian," said Logan.

Markus hit the brake so hard, both of them jerked forward. Luckily, they had their seatbelts on. "What did you say?"

"It's the strangest thing," said Logan. "I don't believe the Guardian would harm us, but at the same time, I'm petrified!"

Markus started to move again. "Why did you think Ashley saw our Guardian?" He rubbed his arms. "I've never laid eyes on her. Have you?"

Logan shook his head.

"What exactly did she see?" asked Markus.

"A couple of weeks ago, she saw a pair of feet in the hallway," said Logan.

"Yikes, you're freaking me out," said Markus. "And what happened?"

Logan closed his fist around the cross so hard until the metal cut into the flesh of his palm. "This cross that Sofia bought for me lay on the floor by my chair and the chain was on my lap." Logan found it hard to talk. He gritted his teeth. "Remember the day I blasted Mom?"

"How could I forget," said Markus. "You were so mad."

Logan removed his hand from the cross. The pain in his palm couldn't compare to the pain he was feeling inside. "The Guardian came to Sofia's home twice."

Markus wrapped his free hand around his neck. "Mom has indeed gone too far."

Logan shook his head. "It happened again tonight!"

"Was your cross on the floor again?" asked Markus.

"Sure was," said Logan.

"Okay, we have to stop Mom," said Markus. "How do we do this?"

Logan stared at the moon. The stars around it twinkled. Without thinking, he touched his cross. "Show us the way," he whispered. "Clear the path for us."

Nineteen

Markus drove passed the farm. Logan turned toward his Old Friend, the Yew tree.

As if reading Logan's mind, Markus said, "It's too late. We'll go tomorrow."

Logan smiled. "You know me too well."

"You're my brother," said Markus.

As they entered the driveway, the lights were still on in the house. Logan glanced at the clock. It was close to 11 P.M.

"Why are they still awake?" asked Logan.

"I was thinking the same thing," said Markus. "Do you think they're expecting us?" He slowed way down.

"Either way, we must stop Mom from interfering with our lives," said Logan.

Markus parked a little farther from the house. He stopped next to the hedges along the driveway. But it was fruitless. The light on the porch came on.

"I dare not go inside, Logan," said Markus.

They sat in the car in silence and stared at their home for five long minutes.

After his anger died down a bit, Logan let out a sigh. "All right, let's get this done and over with."

Markus nodded and opened the door. Logan followed suit. They both staggered toward the house and they clambered up the stairs like sloths. The door flung open. Logan held his breath. His mother appeared at the doorway.

"Omigosh," said Markus. "You scared me, Mom."

His mother held the door open.

"How did you know we were coming home?" asked Logan. "Did the Guardian tell you?"

His mother didn't respond. Her silence pierced Logan's soul. Logan and Markus dragged their feet inside.

"Before you two start lashing out, I want to say something," she said.

Logan and Markus stood in living room. His father stood in the hallway a few feet behind his mother.

"I'm sorry," she said.

Logan spun toward her. His breathing halted. Did he hear it right? Did his mother just apologize?

His mother looked at Markus and then landed her gaze upon Logan. "The Guardian will not step foot at the Flynns again."

Logan inhaled deeply. Markus let out a sigh of relief.

His mother cleared her throat. "Tell Ashley she won. She stands victorious."

Logan blinked. "Huh?"

She shrugged. "That's what the Guardian said. Please relay it to her."

"How could you, Mom?" asked Logan.

His mother sat down.

"Did you send the Guardian, Mom?" asked Markus.

His mother ignored Markus and eyed the cross hanging around Logan's neck. "The Guardian chose you, Logan, to take over my place."

Logan's legs wobbled. He dropped to his knees. His father came flying into the living room and knelt beside him. His father and Markus helped him to the couch.

Logan buried his face in his hands. His head spun. The content of his stomach hurled up toward his nose. He covered his mouth. A tear rolled down his face. "I can't, Mom."

"I know that," she said. "You don't have to."

Logan looked up. Did he hear it right? "Mom…" His voice cracked, he barely recognized it.

"I can't either, Mom," said Markus.

His mother turned toward Markus. "The Guardian didn't have any interest in you or Laurel."

"Arlette!" cried his father.

"I'm laying it all out," said his mother. "No more secrets." His mother stood. She wrung her hands. "This will never happen again. You have my word."

Logan wanted to believe her.

His mother pressed her hands on her chest. "I love you, Logan."

Logan's eyes burned. His mother seemed sincere. He hugged his mother. "I love you too, Mom."

She released Logan and turned to Markus. "I love you, Markus."

Markus rushed toward his mother. "I love you too, Mom."

His father wrapped his arms around all of them. The cross swung around and hit Logan's chest.

"Thank you, Jesus," whispered Logan.

Twenty

That night, Logan lay down in his bed with a smile. A heavy weight had been lifted off his body, mind, and soul. Something happened at the Flynns. There was no doubt about that. The relief he felt a moment ago was replaced with a dreadful feeling. He grabbed his phone and wanted to call Sofia. The clock on his phone stared at him, as if asking was he sure about this. It was late. He sent her a message instead.

"I'm home with Markus," he started. "Is everyone okay there?"

A minute went passed. Logan's heart started to break. What if Sofia decided not to talk to him anymore? He pressed at his chest so hard that the cross tore into his skin.

"Please say something," Logan begged in his dark room.

His phone lit up. In a flash, he read it.

"We're okay. How are you?"

Logan typed, "Mom said it's over for real. I'll explain tomorrow. I'm sorry, Sofia, for what happened."

This time, Sofia's reply was prompt. "We'll talk tomorrow okay. I'm in Ashley's room. Get some sleep."

Logan responded, "Good night."

The next morning, his family acted as if nothing strange had happened the night before. His mother was in the kitchen. The door to The Room was closed.

His mother smiled when Logan walked in. "Good morning, Logan."

Logan smiled back. "Good morning, Mom." He kissed her cheek. "Good morning, Dad."

His father nodded and took a sip of his coffee. "Good morning," his dad mumbled under his breath.

Markus was nowhere to be seen. He must still be sleeping. Logan sat down and smelled the hazelnut coffee before taking a sip. They talked about the weather and the crops.

When he had finished his breakfast, his mother spoke. "Are you going to the Flynns?"

Logan nodded. "They were pretty freaked out last night."

His mother nodded. "I'm sorry. Please tell them that. I swear on your grandmother's grave that it will never happen again."

His father nodded with a smile. For some reason, Logan believed her this time. Perhaps his father's smile assured him.

"Tell them I'm sorry," his mother repeated.

"I will, Mom," said Logan. He left the kitchen and spun around. "I forgot I don't have my car. Markus picked me up last night."

At that exact moment, Markus stepped out of his room. "Give me a few minutes. I'll drive you." He rushed into the kitchen and grabbed a piece of toast. "Let's go."

Logan held out his arms. "Whoa… you better sit down and eat. I'll wait for you by the Yew tree."

Markus scratched his head. "All right. See you in a bit."

His father stood. "I'll drive you there. I have some work I have to do in the field."

Logan kissed his mother's cheek. "See you later, Mom. Love you."

"I love you too," said his mother.

Logan ruffled his brother's hair and ran out before Markus could throw his bread at him. He laughed as he dashed out the door. His father joined his laughter and started the truck.

"I'm sorry about your mother," his father said. "I should have stepped in long time ago."

"What made her change her mind?" asked Logan.

"I don't know," he said. "Last night, she rushed into The Room and came out in a trance. She cried for a second, then stopped. Then, sobbed. It went on like that for like an hour. Then, she returned to The Room. When she came out, she closed the door, and she hasn't been in there since."

"I wonder if it had something to do with Ashley," said Logan. "I hope the Guardian would not hurt her and her family."

"I don't think so," his father said. "She told me last night, when you boys went to bed, that she has decided to let her niece be the Keeper of the Guardian."

"It's more like the Guardian will be the keeper of her," said Logan. "Poor Daisy. Can this be stopped forever, Dad?"

His father shook his head. "I don't think so, and I wouldn't dare try. The Guardian has been in the family for centuries."

"How did you live with this?" asked Logan.

His father smiled. "I love your mother, Logan. I accepted her belief and she accepted mine."

Logan felt warm inside. His mother respected his father's belief. In return, his father respected hers. He wondered if Sofia would accept him if he chose to be an animist like his mother. He felt the cross on his chest.

"Not in a million years," he said to himself and smiled. Then again, he wouldn't want it any other way.

Twenty-One

Ashley stayed up most of the night to make sure nothing was lurking around. Most of all, she was worried about Sofia. Would she stop seeing Logan? Ashley liked the guy. But the mysterious woman had a strong bond to his family. No doubt about that. Although the woman did not harm Logan or them, Ashley feared one of these days… or nights, she might. This must stop.

That morning, Sofia woke up and went back to her room. After a few minutes, she returned and paced Ashley's room. "I'm still scared, Ashley."

"I understand," said Ashley. "But do you love Logan?"

Sofia spun toward her. "I…"

"Dive deep inside your soul," said Ashley. "What did your heart say?"

"If this keeps happening, I can't do it," said Sofia. "I don't want to live in fear my whole life."

Ashley nodded. "I totally understand."

Sofia plopped down on the bed. "This is hard. We come from two different worlds. Sometimes, love is just not enough."

Sofia made a great point.

"You're right," said Ashley. "Yes, our two worlds have collided. So far, the experience hasn't been pleasant, but in the end, it's up to you and Logan to either conquer this or call it quits."

"This is horrible," said Sofia.

"Why don't you think about it and talk to Logan when he comes," said Ashley.

"What makes you think he'll come back?" asked Sofia.

"I don't think he's a quitter, Sofia," said Ashley. "Besides, he left his car here."

Sofia smiled.

"The ball is in your court," said Ashley. "You're in charge."

Sofia made a face. "I don't feel like I am." She rolled from the bed. "I'm going to take a shower."

"See you in a bit," said Ashley. "Everything will be okay."

"Thanks, Ashley," said Sofia. "You're the best."

While Sofia was taking her shower, Ashley lit up the candles and said her prayers. Just like clockwork, Logan came knocking at the front door. Her parents let him in. Ashley finished her prayers, but stayed in her room until someone tapped on her door.

"Ashley, are you in there?" asked Logan.

Ashley smiled. That was a silly question. She opened the door. "Good morning, Logan."

Logan scratched his temple. "Hi, can I come in?"

Sofia leaned forward so Ashley could see her.

Ashley felt Logan had something big to talk to her about, but she had no desire to do it in her room. This was her sacred ground. "Let's go to the living room."

"Okay," said Logan.

Ashley glanced over her shoulder at the altar. The candle flickered. She walked toward the altar and stared at the picture of Jesus and Mother Mary. "*Abide with me*," she whispered in her heart and blew out the candle.

In the living room, Logan looked at every one of them and touched his chest. "From the bottom of my heart, I'm really sorry for what happened."

Ashley's mother let out a low sigh. "You didn't do anything wrong, Logan. Your presence brought us joy."

Logan's eyes glittered. "Thank you, Beth."

"You're my best friend's brother," said Jason. "No ghost or spirit can break the bond we have."

Ashley winced.

Logan smiled. "I spoke with my mother last night. She promised the Guar…" He turned to

Ashley. "Whatever you saw, Ashley, would not come back." He faced Sofia. "I know this happened three times now, but the Guardian—"

"The Guardian?" repeated Jason.

Sofia gasped. Blood drained from Logan's face.

"Markus told me about this before," said Jason. "The jar in the back room."

Logan avoided their gaze and nodded.

"Have you seen her?" asked Jason. He sounded so excited.

"No," said Logan.

"What is this Guardian?" asked Sofia.

Ashley watched Logan fumble. "Logan, I believe you," she said.

"How can you be so sure?" asked Sofia.

Logan straightened and blurted, "The Guardian said Ashely won." He faced Ashley. "You stand victorious. She'll never step foot in this house ever again."

Jason whistled. "Wow, I can't believe the Guardian came here."

"You're happy about this?" asked Sofia.

"The Guardian is cool," said Jason. "She protects the family."

Sofia's jaw dropped. She looked as if she was going to blow up.

Ashley felt the air thicken. She must soothe her sister. She didn't want Sofia to make a big mistake. "Sofia, it's all right," she said softly.

That got Sofia's attention. She turned to Jason. "We have our own Guardian Angel. Don't forget that."

Jason's cheeks reddened. "True."

"And I meant it," said Ashley. "I believe Logan. The Guardian will never come here again." She touched Sofia's shoulder. "You have my word."

Sofia opened her mouth but nothing came out.

Ashley remembered the woman gave her a tiny smile and nodded at her as if saying, "*You got me*." Ashley smiled. "Trust me."

Sofia leaned toward her. "You knew something?"

Ashley looked at both Sofia and Logan. Sweat beaded on Logan's face. They needed the assurance more than anyone in the room.

Ashley gave them all a huge smile. "Everything will be okay. Trust me."

Twenty-Two

Sofia still had doubt in Logan, but she trusted her sister. She was horrified about this Guardian, whatever she is. If it wasn't for Ashley's assurance, she was ready to break up with Logan.

"Mom, Dad, Jason, let's go to the barn," said Ashley.

Her parents got up from the couch. "Good idea,' said her mother.

"No," said Sofia. "Logan and I will go for a walk." She headed for the door.

Logan followed Sofia out the front door.

Sofia turned. "Ashley, can you come along?"

Ashley widened her eyes.

Sofia nodded. "Please…"

"Okay," said Ashley.

As soon as they were out of earshot, Logan said, "Sofia, I'm really sorry."

Ashley's words rang in Sofia's ears. "*We have our own Guardian Angel.*"

Sofia said the prayer to her Guardian Angel before she spoke. "I'm scared, Logan."

"So am I," said Logan.

"What is this Guardian?" asked Sofia. "I can't…"

Logan held Sofia's hands. "My mother has chosen my cousin as the Keeper of the Guardian. It will never come in between us."

Sofia's head spun like a tornado. *What Keeper*?

Logan's eyes glistened with tears. "I know how you feel." His voice cracked. "If I were you, I wouldn't want to see me anymore."

Sofia's lips quivered. "That's not what I meant, Logan."

Logan squeezed her hands. "I don't want to hurt you EVER. I didn't plan for this to happen."

"I know that," she whispered.

Ashley took a few steps back.

Logan stared into Sofia's eyes. "When I told you I'd never hurt you, I meant it. Sofia. I told my mom I've no interest in the family Guardian. And she agreed to assign my cousin as the Keeper."

The word Keeper made Sofia's skin crawl. She wanted to run back inside the safety of her home. "What Keeper?" she finally found the courage to ask.

Logan held her hands. "The Guardian will not have a room in our house—"

Sofia froze. He didn't expect Logan to talk about their future this soon.

Logan must have noticed it as he quickly added, "I can't see myself without you in my life." His chest rose and fell as he went on. "I told my Mom last night I couldn't be the Keeper. The Keeper is someone who will take this Guardian into his/her home. My Mom has chosen Daisy, my cousin, as the Keeper. I will never have anything to do with it."

A spiritual battle took place in her being. Sofia closed her eyes, hoping this was all a bad nightmare.

"Something happened last night," said Ashley.

Sofia's eyes flew open. Even Logan spun toward her sister.

"I can't put it into words," said Ashley. "But trust me, the Guardian will not return." She faced Sofia. "You're right. We come from two very different worlds and these two worlds collided in full force." She turned to both Sofia and Logan. "There's no winner or loser here. You can survive this. You really can if you two unite as one. If you two are being truthful, and you have the love for each other, no one and nothing will break your bond."

Sofia was thankful she asked Ashley to come out. At first, she wanted Ashley there when she broke up with Logan.

"Sofia, please believe me," begged Logan. "There will be no Guardian in our lives."

In the deepest of Sofia's soul, she believed him. But most of all, she trusted her sister. "Logan—"

Before Sofia said another word, Logan blurted, "Sofia, I love you."

Sofia froze. Ashley turned her heels and walked away.

Sofia knew they both had strong feelings for each other, but hearing the "L" word hit her to the core. Her own eyes filled with tears. "I love you back."

Logan pulled her in his arms. "I love you, Sofia Flynn."

She could feel Logan's cross on her skin. In an instant, the fear, the anxiety, the uncertainty evaporated.

Sofia mumbled, "I love you, Logan spencer."

Logan released her. Their eyes locked. Yes, she loved him. No Guardian would break their bond. Ever. Logan leaned forward. One little kiss. That sealed their hearts. Their souls became one.

Sofia touched Logan's cross and kissed it. "Thank you," she whispered. "I love you, Jesus."

~ The End ~

God Bless You

Author's Note

We can achieve Peace
if we ask Peace be the Guardian of our actions

We live in a world filled with different cultures and beliefs. But no one is better than the other. Once you and I accept our differences, there is no reason why we can't live in harmony. Our subconscious thoughts and actions need to be fed and nurtured with love and kindness. We must respect all beings, seen and unseen.

Personally, I owe a lot to my parents and grandmother. They taught me to be a good Christian, to love my neighbors and accept everyone as they are. They instilled in me the love to pray. That doesn't mean I didn't read ghost stories or watch horror movies. Throughout the years, I came to realization that not all ghosts or spirits are malicious. Not all attempt to scare people. Not all want to appear to anyone. Most of all, not all look unsightly or spooky. Still, I am still scared of them (Smile). I turn to prayers to shield me from my own fear. Thus, Cross On A Chain came into existence.

With that, a few thanks are in order. First of all, Thank You to each of my family members and friends. Also, thank you to all fellow writers and readers all around the globe. Thank you for your unending support.

A special Thank You to my Super Editor Connie Butts. Thank you for all you do. I couldn't have done this without you.

And as usual, last but never the least, THANK YOU to my Heavenly Father, Jesus, and Holy Spirit. Another heartfelt Thank You to Mother Mary and all Angels and Saints. From the bottom of my heart, Thank You.

P.S. On the next page (pages), I'll include all the prayers mentioned in this book and my other personal favorites. Peace and God Bless!

My Beloved Prayers

A prayer is special and unique
if you say it sincerely from your heart.

~ My Simple Daily Prayer ~

Thank you, Lord,
For blessing me today (tonight),
For protecting me day and night
Lord, watch over me
Thank you, Lord, Good morning (night), Lord.
Amen.

~ Protection of Five Senses ~

Heavenly Father,
please protect my 5 senses:
my sight, hearing, smell, taste and touch
so that I can give you thanks and glory.
I ask this through Jesus Christ, your son.
Amen.

~ Come Holy Spirit ~

Come Holy Spirit, I need you
Come, Sweet Spirit, I pray
Come in your strength and your power
Come in your own special way

~ Guardian Angels ~

Angel of God, my guardian dear,
to whom God's love entrusts me here,
ever this day (night) be at my side
to light and guard,
to rule and guide.
Amen

~ Saint Michael the Archangel ~

Saint Michael, the Archangel,
defend us in battle.
Be our defense
against the wickedness and snares of the devil.
May God rebuke him, we humbly pray
and do you (thou), O Prince of the heavenly host,
by the power of God
cast into hell Satan and all the evil spirits
who prowl through the world
seeking the ruin of souls.
Amen.

~ Memorare ~

Remember, O most gracious Virgin Mary,
that never was it known
that anyone who fled to your protection,
implored your help or sought your intercession,
was left unaided.
Inspired with this confidence,
I fly to you, O Virgin of virgins, my Mother;
to you do I come, before you I stand,
sinful and sorrowful.
O Mother of the Word Incarnate,
despise not my petitions,
but in your mercy hear and answer me.
Amen.

~ Saint Therese the Little Flower (Saint Therese de Lisieux) ~

(Prayer of petition)

Saint Therese the Little Flower
Please pick me a rose from the heavenly garden,
and send it to me with a message of love.
Ask God to grant me the favor I thee implore
and tell him I will love him
each day more and more.

(Add 5 Our Father, 5 Hail Mary, and 5 Glory be, to be said on 5 successive days before 11 a.m. On the 5th day, offer one more set: 5 Our Father, 5 Hail Mary, and 5 Glory Be)

~ Saint Jude ~

(Prayer of petition)

Most holy Apostle, St. Jude,
faithful servant and friend of Jesus,
the Church honors and invokes you universally,
as the patron of hopeless cases,
of things almost despaired of.
Pray for me, I am so helpless and alone.
Make us I implore you,
of that particular privilege given to you,
to bring visible and speedy help
where help is almost despaired of.
Come to my assistance in this great need
that I may receive the consolation
and help of Heaven
in all my necessities, tribulation, and sufferings,
particularly (state request)
and that I may praise God with you
and all the elect forever.
I promise, O blessed St. Jude,
to be ever mindful of this great favor,
to always honor you
as my special and powerful patron,
and to gratefully encourage devotion to you.
Amen.

~ Saint Joseph ~

(Say for nine mornings in a row for anything you may desire. It has never been known to fail.)

Oh, St. Joseph, whose protection is so great,
so prompt, so strong, before the throne of God,
I place in you all my interests and desires.
Oh, St. Joseph,
do assist me by your powerful intercession,
and obtain for me from your Divine Son
all spiritual blessings,
through Jesus Christ, our Lord.
So that, having engaged here below
your heavenly power,
I may offer my thanksgiving and homage
to the most Loving of Fathers.
Oh, St. Joseph,
I never weary contemplating you
and Jesus asleep in your arms;
I dare not approach
while He reposes near your heart.
Press Him in my name
and kiss His fine Head for me and
Ask Him to return the Kiss
when I draw my dying breath.
St. Joseph, Patron of departed souls - pray for me
Amen.

~ Saint Anthony of Padua ~

O Holy Saint Anthony, gentlest of Saints,
your love for God and Charity for His creatures,
made you worthy, when on earth,
to possess miraculous powers.
Encouraged by this thought,
I implore you to obtain for me [request].
O gentle and loving Saint Anthony,
whose heart was ever full of human sympathy,
whisper my petition into the ears of the sweet Infant Jesus,
who loved to be folded in your arms,
and the gratitude of my heart will ever be yours.
Amen.

(1 Our Father, 1 Hail Mary, 1 Glory Be)

~ Holy Rosary ~

1. Sign of the Cross
   & I Believe (Apostles' Creed)

2. Our Father

3. Three (3) Hail Mary

4. Glory Be
   Fatima Prayer
   Announce the "Mystery"
   Our Father

10. Ten (10) Hail Mary

11. END
   Glory Be
   Fatima Prayer
   Hail Holy Queen

How to say the Rosary

† Sign of The Cross †

In the name of the Father, and of the Son, and of the Holy Spirit, Amen

~ I Believe (Apostles' Creed) ~

I believe in God, the Father almighty,
Creator of heaven and earth,
and in Jesus Christ, his only Son,
our Lord,
who was conceived
by the Holy Spirit,
born of the Virgin Mary,
suffered under Pontius Pilate,
was crucified, died and was buried;
he descended into hell;
on the third day he rose again
from the dead;
he ascended into heaven,
and is seated at the right hand
of God the Father almighty;
from there he will come to judge
the living and the dead.
I believe in the Holy Spirit,
the holy catholic Church,
the communion of saints,
the forgiveness of sins,
the resurrection of the body,
and life everlasting. Amen.

~ Our Father ~
(Traditional version)

Our Father, Who art in heaven
Hallowed be Thy Name;
Thy kingdom come,
Thy will be done,
on earth as it is in heaven.
Give us this day our daily bread,
and forgive us our trespasses,
as we forgive those who trespass against us;
and lead us not into temptation,
but deliver us from evil. Amen.

~ Our Father ~
(Newer version)

Our Father, who is in heaven,
Holy is Your Name;
Your kingdom come,
Your will be done,
on earth as it is in heaven.
Give us this day our daily bread,
and forgive us our sins,
as we forgive those who sin against us;
and lead us not into temptation,
but deliver us from evil. Amen.

~ **Hail Mary** ~
(Traditional version)

Hail Mary full of Grace, the Lord is with thee.
Blessed are thou amongst women
and blessed is the fruit of thy womb Jesus.
Holy Mary Mother of God,
pray for us sinners now
and at the hour of our death
Amen.

~ **Hail Mary** ~
(Newer version)

Hail Mary, full of grace, the Lord is with you.
Blessed are you among women,
and blessed is the fruit of your womb, Jesus.
Holy Mary, Mother of God,
pray for us sinners,
now and at the hour of our death.
Amen.

~ Glory Be ~

Glory be to the Father,
and to the Son,
and to the Holy Spirit.
As it was in the beginning,
is now, and ever shall be,
world without end.
Amen.

~ Fatima Prayer ~

O my Jesus,
forgive us our sins,
save us from the fires of hell,
lead all souls to Heaven,
especially those most in need of Thy mercy.
Amen.

The Mysteries of the Holy Rosary

Monday	Joyful
Tuesday	Sorrowful
Wednesday	Glorious
Thursday	Luminous
Friday	Sorrowful
Saturday	Joyful
Sunday	Glorious (*)

Joyful Mysteries

(Mondays and Saturdays)

* May be said on Sundays during Advent and Christmas

1. The Annunciation
2. The Visitation
3. The Nativity
4. The Presentation
5. The Finding of Jesus in the Temple

Sorrowful Mysteries

(Tuesdays and Fridays)

* May be said on Sundays during Lent

1. The Agony in the Garden
2. The Scourging at the Pillar
3. The Crowning with Thorns
4. The Carrying of the Cross
5. The Crucifixion

Luminous Mysteries
(Thursdays)
1. The Baptism in the Jordan
2. The Wedding at Cana
3. Proclamation of the Kingdom
4. The Transfiguration
5. Institution of the Eucharist

Glorious Mysteries
(Wednesdays and Sundays)
1. The Resurrection
2. The Ascension
3. The Descent of the Holy Spirit
4. The Assumption of the Blessed Virgin Mary
5. The Coronation of the Blessed Virgin Mary

~ Hail Holy Queen ~

Hail, holy Queen, Mother of mercy,
hail, our life, our sweetness and our hope.
To thee do we cry,
poor banished children of Eve,
to thee do we send up our sighs,
mourning and weeping in this vale of tears.
Turn then, most gracious Advocate,
thine eyes of mercy toward us,
and after this our exile,
show unto us the blessed fruit of thy womb, Jesus,
O merciful, O loving, O sweet Virgin Mary!
Amen.

www.ingramcontent.com/pod-product-compliance
Lightning Source LLC
La Vergne TN
LVHW041043150826
845672LV00001B/453

* 9 7 9 8 6 6 3 6 9 1 9 9 4 *